I Can Ride!

by LYNN MASLEN KERTELL
illustrated by SUE HENDRA

SCHOLASTIC INC.

Thank you to Uncle David, for helping Brynn learn to ride.

ISBN 978-0-545-38272-4

10 9 8 7 6 5 4 3 2 1

12 13 14 15 16 17/C

Designed by Angela Jun
Printed in the U.S.A.
First printing, September 2012

40

It is a beautiful day.
"We can all go on a bike ride,"
says Dad.

Anna is a good bike rider.

She pedals at the park.

She goes up and down hills.

Dad says, "Jack, you can go with me."

"I want to ride on two wheels," says Jack.

"Okay, we can try,"
says Dad.

Dad gets his tools.

Dad takes the little wheels
off Jack's bike.

The bike is hard to ride.
The bike wobbles.

The bike falls.
Jack cannot ride the bike.

Dad says, "Jack, I will help you."
Dad takes Jack to a big lot.

The land is smooth and flat.
The ground is black and hard.

Dad holds on to the back of the bike.

The bike wobbles.
The bike skids.

Jack is scared.

Dad says, "Do not give up, Jack.
We can try at the park."

Dad and Jack go up a small hill.
Dad says, "You can do it, Jack."

Jack sits on the bike.

He puts his feet on the ground.

Then he lifts his feet.

The bike does not wobble.

The bike does not tip.

Jack glides down the small hill.

Jack rolls down the hill again and again and again.

Next, Jack puts his feet on the pedals.

His feet push.

The pedals spin.

The bike goes and goes.

"Dad! I did it!" shouts Jack.

Jack rides in the park.
He goes around a bend.

He stops. He starts.
Jack is a bike rider!

Jack calls Grandma. He tells her the good news.

Grandma has a surprise for Jack.

"Now you are a bike rider.
We can all go together!"
says Grandma.

"Yippee!" yells Jack as he pedals away.